ESCAPE FROM PLANET
ALCATRAZ

DIAMONDS OF DOOM

BY MICHAEL DAHL

ILLUSTRATED BY PATRICIO CLAREY

STONE ARCH BOOKS
a capstone imprint

Escape from Planet Alcatraz is published by
Stone Arch Books, an imprint of Capstone.
1710 Roe Crest Drive
North Mankato, Minnesota 56003
www.capstonepub.com

Library of Congress Cataloging-in-Publication Data is available on
the Library of Congress website.
ISBN: 978-1-4965-8675-9 (hardcover)
ISBN: 978-1-4965-9303-0 (paperback)
ISBN: 978-1-4965-8676-6 (ebook pdf)

Summary: One night, Zak Nine and Erro follow a shadowy figure into
a cave in the mountains. Inside they discover the cave is full of priceless
diamonds—and a gang of escaped prisoners. When the Planet Alcatraz
guards arrive, things quickly become dangerous, and the boys have to
rely on each other to find a way out.

Editor: Aaron J. Sautter
Designer: Kay Fraser
Production Specialist: Tori Abraham

Design elements: Shutterstock: Agustina Camilion, A-Star, Dima Zel,
Draw_Wing_Zen, Hybrid_Graphics, Metallic Citizen

Printed and bound in the United States of America.
PA100

TABLE OF CONTENTS

ERRO

PLATEAU of LENG

PHANTOM FOREST

POISON SEA

VULCAN MOUNTAINS

LAKE of GOLD

METAL MOON

DIAMOND MINES

MONSTER ZOO

PITS OF NO RETURN

PRISON STRONGHOLDS

SWAMP OF FLAME

SCARLET JUNGLE

PRISON ENERGY DRIVES

SPACE PORT PRISONER INTAKE

ABYSS OF GIANTS

ZAK

THE PRISONERS

ZAK NINE

Zak is a teenage boy from Earth Base Zeta. He dreams of piloting a star fighter one day. Zak is very brave and is a quick thinker. But his enthusiasm often leads him into trouble.

ERRO

Erro is a teenage furling from the planet Quom. He has the fur, long tail, sharp eyes, and claws of his species. Erro is often impatient with Zak's reckless ways. But he shares his friend's love of adventure.

THE PRISON PLANET

Alcatraz . . . there is no escape from this terrifying prison planet. It's filled with dungeons, traps, endless deserts, and other dangers. Zak Nine and his alien friend, Erro, are trapped here. They had sneaked onto a ship hoping to see an awesome space battle. But the ship landed on Alcatraz instead. Now they have to work together if they ever hope to escape!

ZAK'S STORY . . . LOST IN THE DARK >>>

Erro and I were trying to find our way to Alcatraz's space port. We hoped to find a ship to escape this awful planet. But then we got lost in some rocky hills. Three nights ago, we saw someone wandering in the darkness. But is it a friend or a foe. . . ? >>>>

CHAPTER ONE:
THE CAVE

We only travel when it's dark. We've been following the stranger for three nights. The shadowy figure is a dark shape gliding among the rocks.

It might be a guard headed toward the space port. Or maybe it's another prisoner. Either way, we hope it can lead us to a way off Alcatraz.

Lucky for us, Erro has a good nose. Even though I can't see the stranger, Erro can still smell him.

"Where's he going now?" I ask.

Erro sniffs the air. "It is gone!" he says. "I do not smell it anymore."

"That's impossible!" I say.

I climb on top of a nearby boulder. I stare into the darkness, trying to find the stranger.

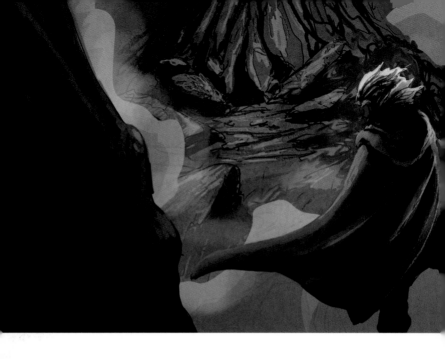

I see a rocky cliff in the distance. There's a dark hole near the bottom.

Erro climbs up beside me, his tail twitching.

"I think he's in that cave," I tell him.

"Maybe it is a she," says Erro. "Or sometimes a he, and other times a she—"

"Okay, okay," I say. "It looked like a he to me."

And I'm sure that he disappeared into that cave.

CHAPTER TWO:
WITHOUT A LIGHT

Erro and I approach the cave
cautiously. Did the stranger know
we were following him? He might be
waiting for us inside.

We carefully step into the darkness.
We can barely see the ground.

But something dim is shining up
ahead of us.

"How can he see in here without a light?" I whisper.

"Maybe he has a good nose like me," whispers Erro.

Soon Erro says, "I can smell him again. Follow me."

It's harder to see the farther we walk inside. I place my hand on the back of Erro's cloak. He leads us into utter darkness.

"OOOOFF!"

I trip over something. Then I slide down a long, smooth slope.

"Erro! Are you there?" I ask.

CHAPTER THREE:
HIDEOUT

"AAAHHHHHHHHH!" I shout as a
bright light hits my eyes.

I rub my eyes and see Erro standing
a few feet from me.

In front of him is an alien holding
a lantern.

But the bright light doesn't come just from the lantern. It's shining all around us.

"Diamonds!" says Erro.

I look around at the cave walls.
Erro is right. The rocks are not
ordinary rocks.

We're surrounded by huge, brilliant
diamonds! They reflect the beam from
the lantern like a thousand mirrors.

"No one remembers this old
diamond mine," says the alien.
"Who sent you here?"

"No one sent us," I say, standing up.

Another, smaller alien steps toward
me. He looks like a blue fish with legs,
wearing dozens of bracelets. I think he's
a Thill, from a planet near my home
Earth base.

"You followed me because the guards sent you!" he says nervously.

"No, wait. We followed you because we thought you knew a way off of Alcatraz," says Erro. "We are escaped prisoners."

"We are all escaped prisoners," says the blue alien.

Suddenly I see several more creatures standing around us.

"We must be careful who we let inside," says the lantern guy. "We don't want the guards to find us."

Ping-Ping-Ping-Ping!

A bracelet on the fishy Thill is glowing and beeping. The lantern guy turns to face him.

"You have betrayed us!" the lantern guy shouts.

CHAPTER FOUR:
DIAMOND DANGER

THOOM! THOOM!

I hear heavy rumbling behind us.

"Surrender!" shouts a deep voice.

"Guards!" yell the aliens.

All of the aliens scatter deeper into the cave—except one.

Wait, why is the Thill just standing there? I ask myself.

As the lantern guy hurries away, the shiny diamonds around us grow darker and darker.

I can still see the Thill's glowing bracelet.

"They're in here!" shouts the Thill.

Suddenly I hear the loud blast of a laser rifle.

ZHHOOOOOOOOM!

Red beams streak through the dark and light up the cave. The dangerous blasts bounce off the shiny diamonds.

Erro and I duck behind some rocks as laser blasts fill the air. They're everywhere!

"Aiiieeeeeh!"

I hear a scream nearby. The blue
Thill has been hit by a laser beam.

"They said they would protect me,"
the fishy alien gasps.

ZHHOOOOM! ZHHOOOOM!

More laser beams cut through the dark.

The diamonds reflect the deadly blasts. The beams cross over our heads in all directions.

"Stop shooting!" I hear a guard cry out. "The reflections could kill all of us!"

CHAPTER FIVE:
UTTER DARKNESS

We're in total darkness. I can't even see my hand in front of my face.

But I can hear the guards marching. They're getting closer.

They're probably wearing night-vision goggles, I think.

"We'll never escape," I say.

"You forget my nose," says Erro in the darkness.

I feel my friend's hand grip my arm.

I hold on to Erro's cloak, and we hurry through the dark as fast as we can.

Erro suddenly stops. I hear him sniff the air.

"I believe the other prisoners have escaped," he says.

Does that mean we can too? I wonder.

The sounds of the guards are far away.

Erro takes the lead, and we walk
through the diamond maze for hours.

Suddenly Erro stops and sniffs again.
Then I sniff too . . . fresh air! Erro has
found the cave's back entrance.

We escape the deadly diamond cave
and run into the night. At least we have
starlight to help us find another place
to hide. . . .

GLOSSARY

betray (bee-TRAY)—to do something that hurts someone who trusts you

boulder (BOHL-dur)—a large rounded rock

brilliant (BRIL-yuhnt)—bright and full of light

cautiously (KAW-shuhs-lee)—doing something very carefully

cloak (KLOHK)—a loose piece of outer clothing; a cape

diamond (DYE-muhnd)—a shiny, precious gemstone; one of the hardest substances known to humans

laser (LAY-zur)—a thin, intense beam of light

night-vision goggles (NITE-VIZH-uhn GOG-uhlz)—advanced eyewear that allows one to see in the dark

reflection (ree-FLEK-shuhn)—the change in direction of light bouncing off a surface

slope (SLOHP)—a slanted surface like a slide or a hillside

species (SPEE-sheez)—a group of living things that share similar features

utter (UHT-ur)—complete or to the extreme

TALK ABOUT IT

1. Erro has a very strong sense of smell. He can track creatures and find his way in the dark using only his nose. Can you think of any creatures on Earth that have this ability?

2. The diamonds inside the cave reflect light and laser blasts in all directions. Why do you think they do this? What quality of diamonds would cause this to happen?

3. After Zak and Erro get away from the Alcatraz guards, they rely on Erro's nose to find a way through the dark cave. Can you think of another way the boys could have found a way out? Explain your answer.

WRITE ABOUT IT

1. After Zak and Erro enter the cave, they meet several alien prisoners. Write a short story describing how the aliens know each other and why they are hiding in the cave.

2. Imagine that you are the fishy Thill alien. Why would you wear a tracking device for the guards to find you? Write down why you would do this and why you believe the guards would protect you.

ABOUT THE AUTHOR

Michael Dahl is the author of more than 300 books for young readers, including the bestselling Library of Doom series. He is a huge fan of Star Trek, Star Wars, and Doctor Who. He has a fear of closed-in spaces, but has visited several prisons, dungeons, and strongholds, both ancient and modern. He made a daring escape from each one. Luckily, the guards still haven't found him.

ABOUT THE ILLUSTRATOR

Patricio Clarey was born in 1978 in Argentina. He graduated in fine arts at the School of Visual Arts Martín Malharro, specializing in illustration and graphic design. Patricio currently lives in Barcelona, Spain, where he works as a freelance graphic designer and illustrator. He has created several comics and graphic novels, and his work has been featured in several books and other publications. Patricio is working on launching his first art book, *Attractor*.